PEANUTS®

Merry Christmas, Charlie Brown

ILLUSTRATED BY CHARLES M. SCHULZ CREATIVE ASSOCIATES

we make books come alive™

pi kids® **Phoenix International Publications, Inc.**

Chicago • London • New York • Hamburg • Mexico City • Paris • Sydney

WHEN CHARLIE BROWN GOES SKATING, HIS DOG SNOOPY JOINS IN, TOO. SEARCH THROUGH THE SKATERS TO FIND SOME OF THEIR WINTER WEAR:

THIS SCARF

THESE GLOVES

THIS HAT

THESE GLOVES

THIS HAT

THIS SHIRT

WHEN CHARLIE BROWN NEEDS MONEY TO BUY PEGGY JEAN A PRESENT, HE DECIDES TO SELL HIS COMIC BOOK COLLECTION. SEARCH THROUGH THE STACKS TO FIND SOME OF CHARLIE BROWN'S OLD FAVORITES:

"THIS LITTLE GREEN ONE HERE SEEMS TO NEED A HOME," SAYS CHARLIE BROWN. LOOK FOR SOME OTHER CHRISTMAS TREES THAT ARE MUCH MORE COLORFUL:

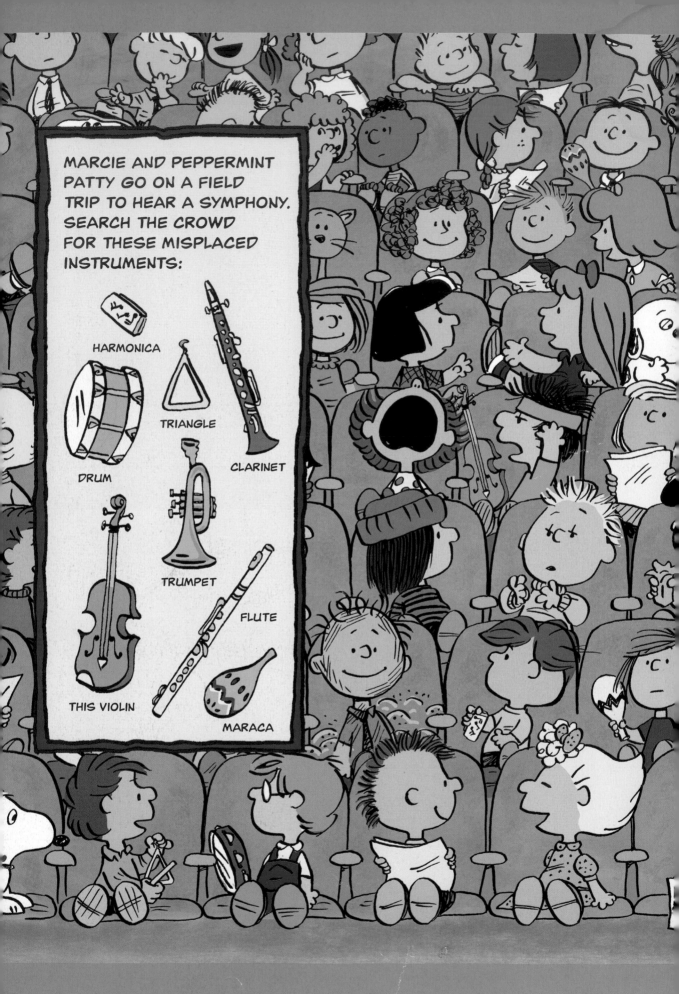

MARCIE AND PEPPERMINT PATTY GO ON A FIELD TRIP TO HEAR A SYMPHONY. SEARCH THE CROWD FOR THESE MISPLACED INSTRUMENTS:

HARMONICA

TRIANGLE

CLARINET

DRUM

TRUMPET

FLUTE

THIS VIOLIN

MARACA

"LOOK! I JUST BOUGHT THIS NEW PAIR OF GLOVES!" SAYS PEGGY JEAN. CHARLIE BROWN'S PLAN IS RUINED. SHOP AROUND THE STORE TO FIND SOME GLOVES HE CONSIDERED BUYING FOR PEGGY JEAN:

TIME TO DECORATE THE TREE! LOOK THROUGH THE BOX TO FIND THESE CHRISTMAS ORNAMENTS:

RETURN TO THE ICE-SKATING PARTY TO FIND THESE KIDS:

GO BACK TO THE LIGHTS & DISPLAY CONTEST TO FIND THESE COLORFUL CANDY CANES:

GO BACK TO THE COMIC BOOK SALE TO FIND THESE OTHER THINGS THAT CHARLIE BROWN TREASURES:

PENNANT

BASEBALL

LUNCHBOX

BASEBALL CARD

THIS HAT

TOY PLANE

RETURN TO THE CHRISTMAS TREE LOT TO FIND CHARLIE BROWN'S CHRISTMAS TREE AND THESE OTHER PLAIN AND SIMPLE THINGS:

ICE SKATES

TOY HOOP

PIE

TOY HORSE

TIN CAN PHONE

SLED

THIS TREE

SOAR BACK TO THE SYMPHONY TO FIND THESE KIDS IN THE AUDIENCE:

- A BOY IN A RED SHIRT SITTING NEXT TO A GIRL WITH CURLS
- A GIRL IN A POLKA-DOTTED DRESS TALKING TO A BOY IN A BLUE SHIRT
- A GIRL IN A BLUE DRESS SITTING NEXT TO TWINS
- A BOY IN A PLAID SHIRT SITTING IN FRONT OF A GIRL IN A GREEN DRESS
- A BOY IN A GREEN SWEATER SITTING NEXT TO A GIRL WITH A PURPLE HAT
- A GIRL IN A PURPLE SHIRT SITTING BETWEEN TWO BOYS

RETURN TO THE DEPARTMENT STORE TO FIND THESE COLORFUL BOTTLES OF PERFUME:

ROLL BACK TO THE BOX FULL OF CHRISTMAS ORNAMENTS TO FIND THESE FESTIVE STICKERS:

RETURN TO THE SNOW DAY TO FIND SOME FAMILIAR-LOOKING SNOW SCULPTURES:

PIANO

DOGHOUSE

FOOTBALL

SNOOPY

WOODSTOCK

CHARLIE BROWN